Very Scary

WITHDRAWN

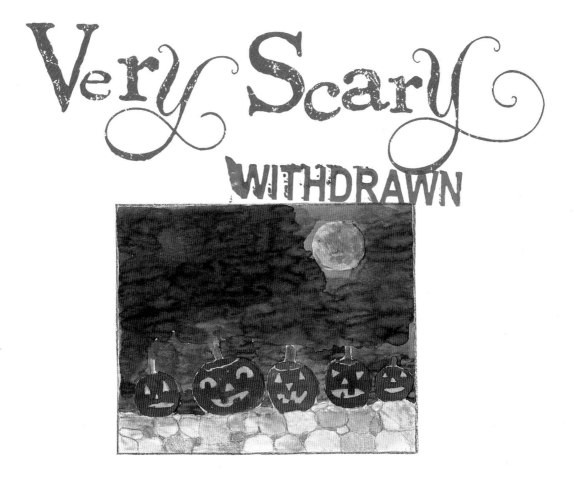

written by Tony Johnston

illustrated by Douglas Florian

Voyager Books
Harcourt Brace & Company
San Diego   New York   London

First Voyager Books edition 1999
Voyager Books is a registered trademark of Harcourt Brace & Company.

The Library of Congress has cataloged the hardcover edition as follows:
Johnston, Tony, 1942–
Very scary/Tony Johnston; illustrated by Douglas Florian.—1st ed.
p. cm.
Summary: A pumpkin shimmering in the moonlight attracts the
attention of an owl, a cat, crickets, a witch, and a group of boys
and girls, who change it into a scary jack-o'-lantern.
ISBN 0-15-293625-4
ISBN 0-15-202097-7 pb
[1. Pumpkin—Fiction.   2. Halloween—Fiction.   3. Jack-o'-lanterns—Fiction.]
I. Florian, Douglas, 1950– ill.   II. Title.
PZ7.J6478Ver   1995
[E]—dc20   94-10938

A   C   E   F   D   B

Printed in Singapore

The illustrations in this book were done in watercolor on vellum paper.
The text type was set in Colwell.
Color separations by Bright Arts, Ltd., Singapore
Printed and bound by Tien Wah Press, Singapore
This book was printed on Arctic matte paper.
Production supervision by Stanley Redfern and Jane Van Gelder
Designed by Lisa Peters

For Dorothy Fenner, San Marino legend,
who taught me that the English language
is really not very scary
—T. J.

For Marvin Bileck
—D. F.

For Dorothy Fenner, San Marino legend,
who taught me that the English language
is really not very scary
—T. J.

For Marvin Bileck
—D. F.

One night the moon was shining, an orange, pumpkin moon. All the pumpkins by the fence shimmered in its light.

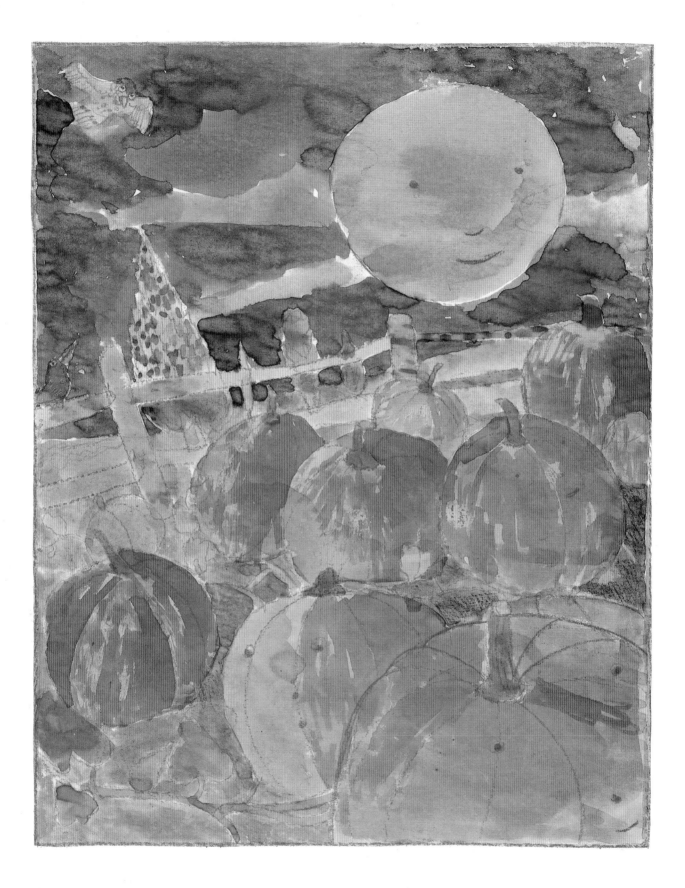

The biggest pumpkin soaked up the light till it felt full of moon.

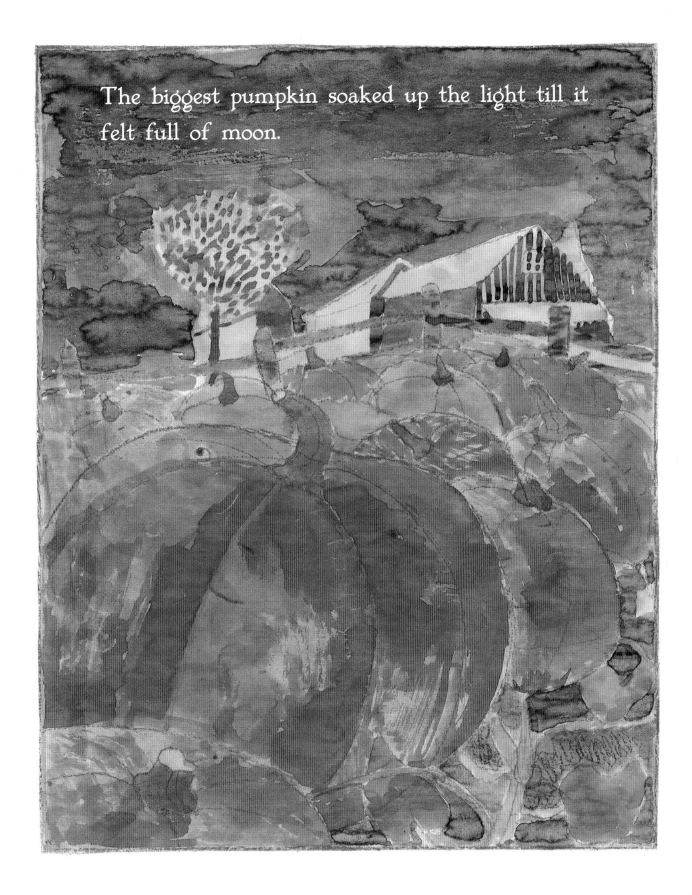

An owl flew down like a brown leaf.
It went *woo-woo-woo* with all its
might because that pumpkin
shined so bright.

A cat came *tiptoe-tiptoe-tiptoe.*
It *purr-purr-purred* with all its might because
that pumpkin shined so bright.

creaky

A little choir of crickets hopped on top of the pumpkin. They sang *creaky-creaky-creaky* with all their might because that pumpkin shined so bright.

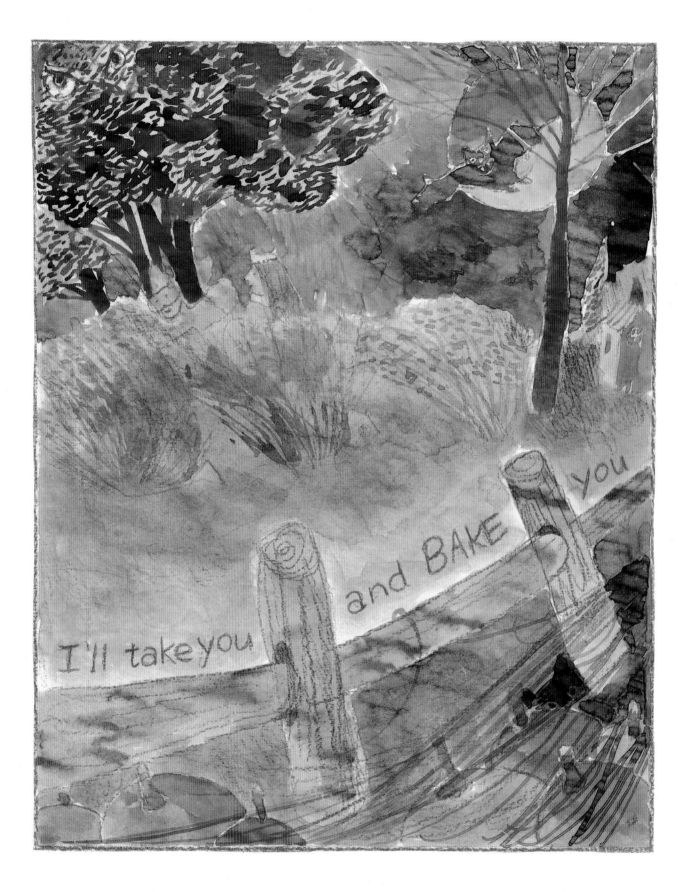

A witch came *sneaky-sneaky-sneaky*.
"I'll take you and bake you," she said. And she gave
it a pat. The pumpkin tried to look very scary.
But it just looked big and FAT. The witch
reached for it. But—

she hid instead. For there came a loud noise. Girls and boys— searching, seeking, peeking.

For what? A pumpkin.
They cried *ooh-ooh-ooh* with all their might
because that pumpkin shined so bright.

A girl drew a face on it. Then they carved it carefully.

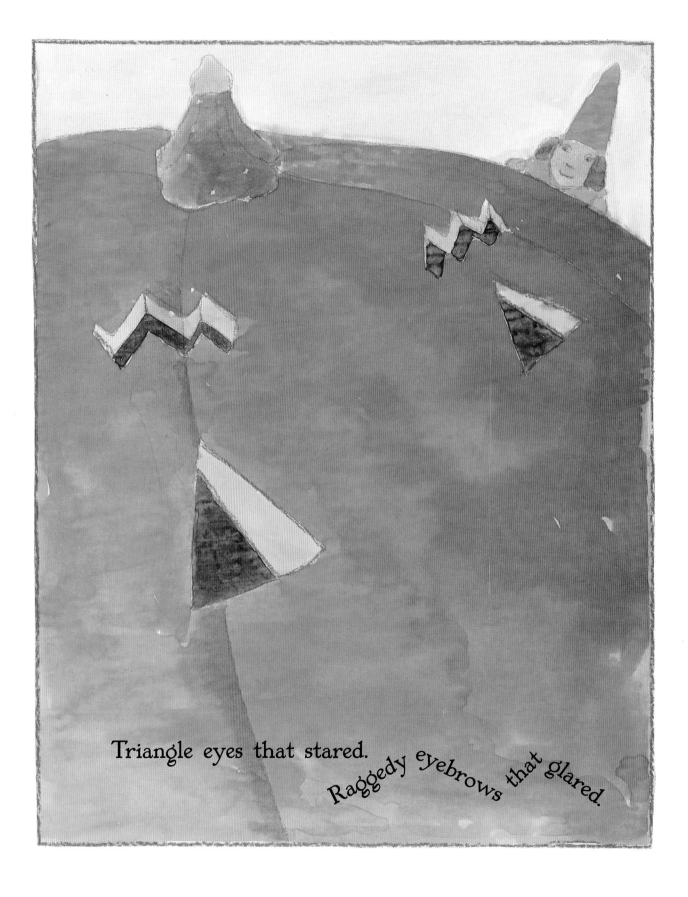

Triangle eyes that stared.

Raggedy eyebrows that glared.

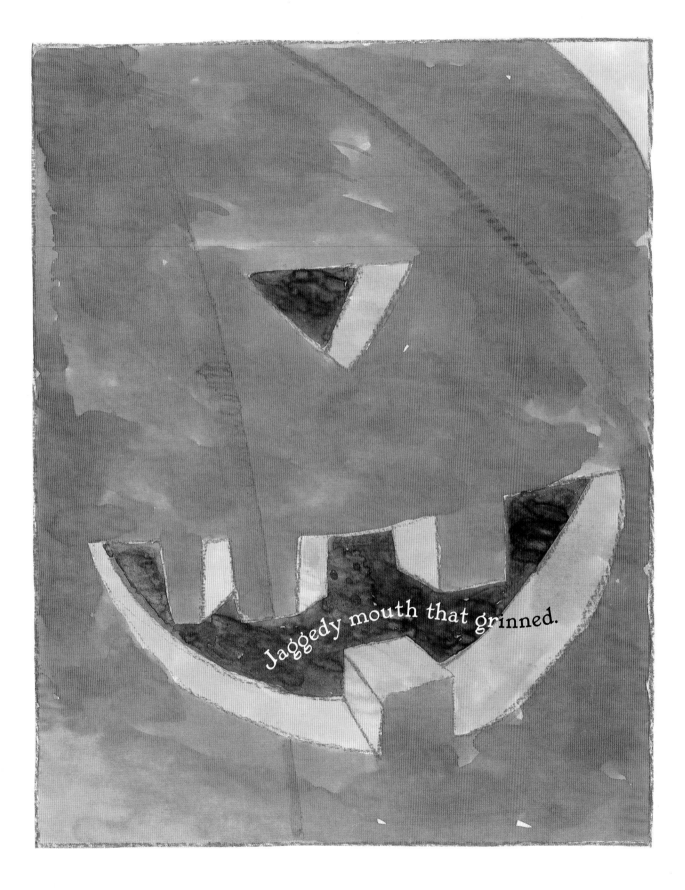

Jaggedy mouth that grinned.

When they stuck a candle in, the pumpkin shouted *BOO!* with all its might.

The owl flew.

The cat fled.

The crickets hurried.

The witch scurried.

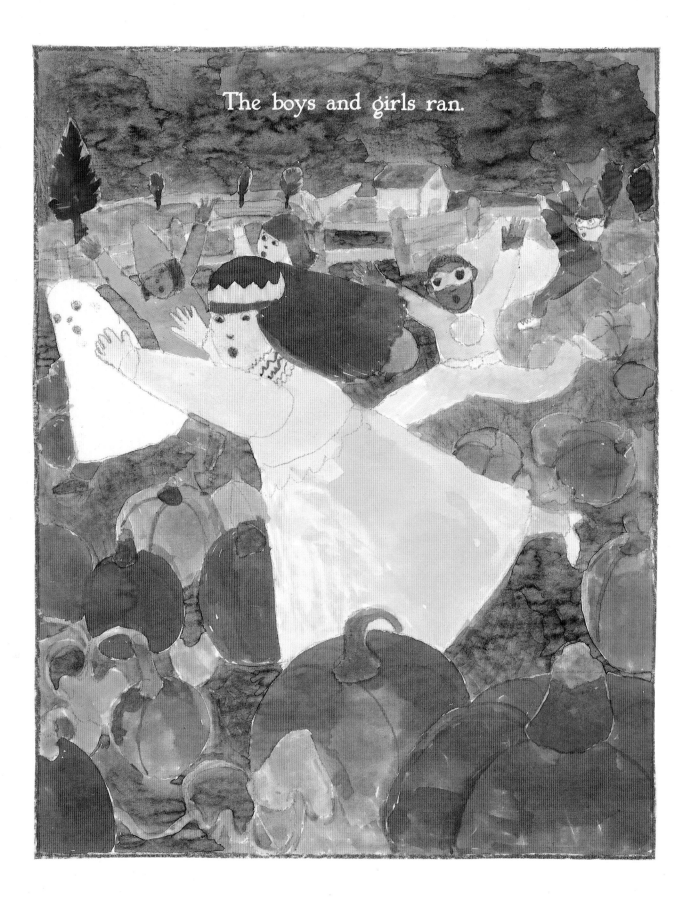

The boys and girls ran.